The Billionaire CEO

Emily Cooper

Romance: The Billionaire CEO

Emily Cooper

Copyright © 2015

Published by Run Free Publishing

All rights reserved.

No part of this publication may be reproduced, stored in a retrieval system, or transmitted, in any form or by any means without the prior permission in writing of the publisher.

This is a work of fiction. Any resemblance to any person, living or dead, is purely coincidental.

Other titles by bestselling author Emily Cooper:

Romance: Seduced by the Billionaire's Lust

Romance: The Billionaire's Assistant

Romance: Bought for the Billionaire's Pleasure

Romance: Alpha Stepbrother

Romance: The Billionaire Proposal

Romance: The Assistant

The Billionaire CEO

Emily Cooper

1

So today is the day.

As I step through the revolving doors of the dreary grey building, I have a clear purpose in mind.

Today is the day.

For the last four years I've worked as a journalist for *Leading Edge Press,* a popular printed and online news publication that is currently in its tenth year of operation.

As I walk through the building, I see a thriving workplace filled with diverse furnishings and enthusiastic employees. The inside of this building is a stark contrast to the outside.

From its perky red retro chairs, to its stark white tables, to its alien-like designed computer pods, and lime green sofas - where all news writers are encouraged to sit and find their "inner inspiration" - the whole floor screams a modern twist on the 60s era. It's like Andy Warhol walked in and went crazy – bright colors and stenciled canvases catching your eye from almost every viewpoint.

It's a mecca for artsy types, and that's a large part of the reason why I love my job so much.

As a fine art graduate from NYU my two passions meld here, words meeting images in epic utilitarianism.

Leading Edge Press has published hundreds of my stories, from my humbler beginnings as the resident '*How To*' girl, followed by a stint of reporting on Manhattan's most trendy hotspots, and now my most recent promotion as a more serious journalist.

My career highlights have been on the back of tough investigative journalism into how billionaire bachelor Jackson Windsor has been destroying lives through his African diamond mines. I was up to my third hard-hitting article on the handsome man when he completely disappeared off the map.

After the success of my brutal articles, I have had my pick of hard-hitting stories - whether it's highlighting political scandals, detailing the latest breakthroughs in medicine and science, or investigating controversial foreign affairs.

That is until Hank McAllister tips the scales yet again. He often rips my feature articles into shreds and demands they be rewritten with less *"emotional attachment."*

But today is the day.

Hank is a product of the "baby boomer" generation. He doesn't believe in climate change, gay marriage, feminism or environmental groups.

"Radical hippy, left winged jargon" he calls all of it. *"Turning the world into even more of a backward place than it already was to begin with!"*

And even though he's been a news editor for twenty odd years, he still doesn't understand the evolution of journalism over that time, a movement that no longer shies away from uncovering the darker facts, no matter how shocking they might be.

If he wants a story on Jackson Windsor's illegal diamond mining in Zimbabwe with forced labor and torture camps, then he should be prepared for the gritty facts, not an innocuously polished article with a few comments from the heads of mining companies swearing that nothing criminal ever happens under their jurisdiction.

After all, where's the truth and journalism in that?

I don't know why Hank chose to be the publishing supervisor here.

He's nothing like the rest of us writers, and he hates the kind of stories we churn out to our readers. But he's a brilliant editor; I need to credit him with that much.

Even if you write the crappiest and most unprintable story, once he's finished with it and blasted you about all the things you need to change, it comes out as good as gold. When he's not being an arrogant son of a bitch, he's almost respectable.

I stroll into Hank's office with my head held high, steady breaths and rehearsed speech, but as soon as I see his shiny bald head look up at me all my confidence just melts away.

Today has to be the day...

I have decided today is when I finally tell my prick boss of an editor to stick his chauvinism where the sun doesn't shine.

"Ah, Claire!" he bellows as I walk in. "Sit! I have a new assignment for you. Scrap that last story you did. This is better!"

"What? But I was up all night finishing it," I protest, sinking down into the chair opposite him. I'd stayed up until three a.m. editing the final draft of my feature article on the torture camps in the Middle East.

Surely he's not suggesting I get rid of it completely?

"Tough. I want a different angle now," he huffs. "Besides, there's something big in it for you. And by big, I mean dollar signs, baby!"

Oh man, here we go.

Hank has that gleam in his eye, the one he gets when he's on the verge of catching a big fish. I hate it when he calls me '*baby*' too, like I'm a fine piece of meat that he's been admiring.

I'm twenty-six years old!

"Hank, I told you to stop calling me that," I say sternly, narrowing my eyes on him. "It's not appropri—"

"Oh cool your jets!" he interrupts, refusing to look me in the eye. "Why do you have to be so uptight all the time? Good thing you're one of my best writers, Claire." He stops to take a breath, shuffling some papers in front of him. "Anyway, back to the issue at hand. I need you to interview Jackson Windsor."

He states it matter-of-factly, like it's not even up for discussion.

"Wait, hold up. You want me to interview him?" I ask, screwing my face up at him like he's just made some crude joke.

"Well, unless you know of anyone else worth interviewing...of course I want you to interview him!"

"But he's a famous recluse. He has disappeared off the face of the earth," I laugh. "No one gets to interview him. In fact, no one's heard anything about him for like twelve months."

Hank grins at me keenly. "Exactly. Hence why this is our cash cow, baby!"

"Hank..."

"Alright, alright. I'll curb my tongue on the baby thing. But I'm serious about this, Claire. You have top spot on this one!"

I shake my head at him, still utterly confused.

And to think the only agenda I had in mind for today was calling Hank out on being a sexist pig.

How the hell has he even managed to score this interview?

Jackson Windsor is as untraceable as a ghost, and he doesn't even live in the States.

He lives in some remote part of Canada, hibernating in a lavish log-cabin styled mansion on a stretch of its wild and rugged coastline.

Anyone with a keen interest in celebrities and world news knows the story…

Jackson Windsor became an orphan at fifteen when his famous and rich geologist parents died in a plane crash whilst celebrating their 20th wedding anniversary in the Bahamas. From their estate he inherited a decent fortune, and under the care of his late grandmother, Maggie Windsor, he went on to finish high school. Inspired by his parents work, Windsor decided to point his career in a similar direction and completed an earth and environmental engineering degree at Columbia University. After five years of working as the head of operations for a large mining company, he decided to go one step further, investing two billion dollars into South

African and Zimbabwe mines. However, on his thirtieth birthday, after having only owned the mines for a year, he suddenly announced that he was closing them down for good, but refused to give any reason as to why. Since that day twelve months ago he has avoided all press and people like the plague.

It's one of those cold cased intriguing stories that every journalist wants the scoop on but has never been able to catch.

And that's what I'm apprehensive about.

Even if I do the interview with Jackson Windsor I doubt he's going to come through with the goods—notably the garish details behind why he closed his mines.

There are whispers that he did it to try and quell the marketing of blood diamonds in the region, but having done extensive research on it, and Windsor himself, I know there's more to it than just that.

I think something even more sinister took place.

"So when is this all-exclusive interview supposed to be happening?" I ask sarcastically, widening my eyes at Hank for dramatic effect.

"Friday."

"What? That only gives me one day to prepare!"

"So? Think on your feet. All good journalists know how," he says smugly, brandishing a wink.

Pfft, as if he knows anything about what being a good journalist entails. He might be at the top of his field when it comes to editing news stories, but in terms of actually sitting down and talking to a high profile figure, Hank doesn't know squat. He hasn't done an interview since Reagan was in office.

"Okay...well what hotel in New York is Windsor staying at?"

"None. He won't be in New York."

"Right..." I sigh tetchily. "So it's a phone interview?"

But Hank is grinning like a jackass again. "No. You'll be doing it in person."

I roll my eyes and slump back in the chair. I hate it when he plays games with me like this. Why can't he just spit it out?

"Okay, Hank, I'll play along," I say, clearly frustrated. "How am I supposed to interview this guy if it's not in New York and not by telephone?"

Hank picks up the expensive fountain pen the staff gave him for his birthday last year and points it towards the ceiling. "You ever heard of those big metal things that fly in the sky?" he says smartly, obviously waiting for the penny to drop.

"Wait, you don't mean—"

"First class too. You're lucky the billionaire's paying. We would've just put you in coach!"

But lucky is not exactly how I feel right now.

The expression on my face resembles more of the reaction you have when you're trapped in a fighting ring and have just been given a stunning blow by your opponent.

Often it's been the case with a celebrity like Jackson Windsor that they bail out of the interview at the last minute. Or worse, they give you one that's D.O.A. and utterly boring.

"I'm not asking you to fly to Canada, Claire. I'm telling you to! It's not negotiable. Your flight leaves tomorrow morning. Here!" Hank takes out a large sealed yellow envelope from the top drawer of his desk and throws it onto my lap. "Everything you need is in there. Boarding tickets, travel itinerary, address of his mansion out in whoop whoop. Make sure to keep all your receipts so I can reimburse you for needed expenses. And I mean NEEDED, Claire."

I falter, still trapped in the fighting ring. "And if I refuse?"

"Well, I hear the *'How To'* team could do with an extra contributor."

"You wouldn't dare demote me!" I hiss. But we both know who the snake is and who the mouse in this situation is.

"Try me, blondie. Besides, this is the scoop of the year if not the decade! You know as well as I do that you're not going to turn that down."

Unfortunately, the beefy and red-faced little man is right.

If I manage to find out why Jackson Windsor closed his mines and there's a scandal at the heart of it, then this could propel me right to the top of my career. I could make editor at another publication or magazine, a dream ripe for the taking.

"Fine," I cave, taking the envelope. "I hate how you know me so well sometimes, Hank."

"You're a journalist, Claire, eager to hunt down a good story and put a bullet right between its eyes. You're an open book. We all are. Now, if there isn't anything else you want to complain about, then get going will you! I have to finish red-penning the hell out of these drafts!"

I scowl at him contemptuously and go to leave, turning at the last minute to backtrack a few steps.

"Wait, I just have one more question."

"Of course you do," he sighs heavily, looking up from the piece of paper already marred with several red scribbles.

"How did you land this interview? This could potentially be big. REALLY BIG. And we're not exactly 60 Minutes or Barbara Walters."

"Look, all you need to know is that he reached out to me personally, and he's ready to talk," Hank says firmly, shaking his head at me like I'm a disobedient child. He's told me before that I remind him of his 13-year-old daughter, all lip and attitude yet as savvy and inquisitive about the world as he is.

It's curious that he won't tell me any more details about his correspondence with the billionaire.

I guess I'll just have to get it from the horse's mouth himself on Friday.

If Jackson Windsor is willing to give me a story on the closure of his mines, then surely he can provide me with the link between him and my moronic editor.

"Okay. Can I ask one more thing?"

"Can I stop you?" Hank sniggers, placing a cigar in his mouth.

"No," I say staunchly, cracking a wry smile before continuing on. "So why are you sending me to do the interview? Pete is the main foreign affairs correspondent. He's interviewed a ton of mining company big wigs over the years."

"I told you already. As much as I wish it wasn't so, you're one of my best writers. And you're single. Pete has a wife and kids."

"What has being single got to do with it? It's only a couple of days work. Pete has travelled for a story before."

"Man! There's no pulling the wool over your eyes is there," Hank grunts, a harder frown setting in his face. "Look, the billionaire requested you, okay? End of story."

"He requested me?" I repeat hazily, wondering how on earth Jackson Windsor even knows of me. But then again I have dragged his name through the gutter a few times...but that should deter him from talking to me, not the opposite!

"That's a little odd, don't you think?"

Hank shrugs at the comment. "I don't know. Is it?"

"Yes, considering the things I've said about him in some of my articles."

"Well, maybe he wants to set the record straight...or seduce you to his way of thinking," he jibes, giving out a stout laugh.

"Well, I hope you don't expect me to sleep with him to get the story! Because that's low, even for you, Hank."

"Now don't get cute with me, blue eyes," he warns, the small amount of wit that was in his tone now completely gone. "Whatever you do in your personal life is up to you. But if that just so happens to include sleeping with reclusive billionaires, then hey, I won't stop you. Just get the story! I don't care by what methodology. Ethically or unethically, it's on your moral compass. But have the transcript of the interview and final draft of the story on my desk by this time next week or go join the rookies in *'How To'*," he barks, motioning towards the door with his hand. "Now scoot, you've already wasted enough of my time!"

"Prick," I mutter under my breath as I leave his office, the thick stench of cigar smoke already swirling behind me.

Just typical, Claire. Another successful day of letting Hank walk all over you. When will you ever get the guts to stand up to that guy?

But hey, at least I got a first class ticket to Canada out of it. I'd be lying if I didn't admit that I've always wanted to go there. *Lake Louise…The Rocky Mountains*…a log cabin in the woods by a lake that is as cool to dive under, as it is refreshing…

But Jackson Windsor doesn't live on a lake.

He lives on the coast.

Damn it.

2

When I walk out into the greater office the first thing I see is Sophia waving at me frantically.

Sophia is a petite Spanish girl with warm brown eyes and a cute smile. She also just happens to be my best friend.

"So you're heading to Canada!" she sings out like a soprano, hurrying up to my side.

"You heard, huh? That was fast," I remark, throwing her a questioning look.

"Are you kidding? Who do you think convinced that prick in there to send you?"

"Even after Jackson Windsor requested you, Hank still wanted Pete to go," Sophia adds.

"Are you serious?" I whir at her, growing even madder at Hank, which I didn't think was possible at this point. "I hate him, Sophia! He scrapped my article on the torture camp in the Marange diamond fields. You know how much work and research I put into that."

"Oh, Claire," she says soothingly, rubbing my back. "Look at it this way. If you can get Jackson Windsor to admit the truth behind why he closed down his mines, you'll get more than just a torture camp. It's a can of worms, honey. You just need to lift the lid on it. Jackson Windsor is a cash cow."

"Oh God, you sound like Hank!" I joke. "Where's that lovely little Spaniard gone?"

"Ouch, comparing me to Hank actually hurt a little," she brays jokily before, steering me into the staff lunchroom on our immediate left. "So, do you need a lift to the airport tomorrow?"

"No, I'll catch a cab. I'd rather Hank pay for the petrol," I say with a wide grin that even *The Joker* would be proud of. "He did say it was all expenses paid as long as I keep the receipts."

"Milking it for all its worth, huh?"

"Of course. Unlike you," I tease, jabbing her playfully with my elbow. "You're way too nice to ever financially take advantage of your boss."

She gives me a light pinch on the arm and grabs an apple from the fruit bowl on the lunchroom table.

"Whatever," she sighs, a smirk escaping her lips just before she bounces back out towards the office.

"Oh," she calls back, "And make sure you don't fall in love. He's devastatingly handsome, you know? And has a wicked reputation. There isn't an actress or model he hasn't been able to woo."

"Not a chance," I shout assertively. "I'm into artsy guys, not arrogant billionaire businessmen who are notorious for aiding in the trafficking of blood diamonds."

But Sophia doesn't look convinced. "*Allegedly* notorious," she warns. "And remember that famous saying, honey, '*don't judge a book by its cover.*' You never know what's written in its pages."

After she slinks away I can't help but chuckle over the image of Hank with big pink ears and a fat snout. I turn back around to the coffee machine on the countertop, eager for my first hit of caffeine for the day. As I tamper off the coffee I think back to what Sophia said about falling for Jackson Windsor. *As if that could ever happen to you, Claire,* I scoff in my head. He's like a suit without a soul, the same kind of wolf mentality that they breed them down on Wall Street. And he's the underlying nemesis in several of my articles related to unlawful diamond mining in Zimbabwe. The two of us together would be like Lois Lane ending up with Lex Luthor instead of Superman.

It's completely out of the realms of possibility.

3

The view outside the slick, black rented BMW's window is beyond spectacular.

In fact, every part of Vancouver Island so far has been sweepingly beautiful.

Much of it is protected parkland that is studded with pockets of old growth firs and cedar forests, as well as rare natural groves of Garry Oak. I read that this southern part of the island, not too far from the capital of Victoria yet remote enough so that I haven't seen a single house or car pass me in the last hour, is a nature lover's paradise, with pristine hiking trails, unique pebble beaches and plenty of marshes for bird watching.

"Not that I'll get to explore any of it!" I natter behind the wheel, speaking only to the silence of the car.

I check the map Hank had given me in the yellow envelope, the precise location of Jackson Windsor's mansion represented as a large red dot right on the coastline, about thirty miles from the nearest town of Metchosin.

Although it shouldn't be too much further now, I'm dreading the arrival.

Alone in a remote location with a tall, strong man who I have severely criticized to the public and accused of enforcing slave labor in his diamond mines.

What part of that sentence seems like a wise idea?

After another few miles of curving back roads lined with Blackberry bushes, and with the late summer sun slowly sinking on the horizon, I finally spot the grand waterfront estate sitting high on the cliff's edge.

"Oh," I whisper as I drive through the property's tall wrought iron gates. "This place is huge…"

When I finally come to a stop out front, I squint up in sheer wonderment at the glowing mansion.

Its overall design is unlike anything I've ever seen, distinctly Canadian but abstractly so, with small varying square and rectangular windows scattered across its entire length.

From the outside their positioning seems strange, but the true purpose of the windows is probably for lead light, which will have a greater impact once I'm inside and looking out.

The roof is unusually straight too, except for a sharp peak like a witch's hat pared on the far right.

Just on the architecture alone the value of the property must be at least ten million.

But then again for a billionaire I suppose that's rather cheap.

"The size of this place has to be at least 10,000 square feet," I say, stepping nervously out of the BMW.

But just as I do a great thrust of westerly wind threatens to knock me back in again, the car door swaying rebelliously in my hands.

It's like I have managed to arrive in the middle of a gale force windstorm.

When I finally manage to shut the door, I make my way towards the swirled white marble porch that marks the mansion's entrance.

I knock twice on the solid oak front door, my knuckles reddening under the impact with a few shoots of pain before I notice the doorbell shaped like a leaf on my lower left.

But even after pressing that several times there is still no answer.

What the hell could he be doing in there?

I contemplate getting back in the car and checking in early at the hotel in Metchosin Hank had booked me in for the night, but the thought of delaying the interview until tomorrow and potentially having to reschedule my flight back to New York for Sunday turns me off instantly.

I decide to try my luck around the side, taking care not to damage the intricate landscaped garden of pebbles and strange plants that look like cacti, until a long bay window extending from the second story down to the ground floor comes into view.

Through it I see a grand, chic black dining table and numerous large paintings hanging on the walls, the faint outline of an extravagant open planned kitchen and stunning lounge room further into the house.

Wow.

So this is how the rich and powerful live in seclusion huh?

It's nice.

Very nice.

If only the rest of us could be so lucky!

I continue on towards the rear of the mansion until the obstacle of a river meets me.

Well what appears to be a river, only it's contoured like a manmade canal and runs through the center of the entire house.

Typical.

Even billionaires can confine Mother Nature to their demands.

Heading back around to the front I try the door again, but still no answer.

Finally, I figure I'll just try the handle...

And it opens.

Obviously, Jackson Windsor doesn't care much about security.

But then again, look where I am.

How many people even know this place exists, let alone would be bothered to drive all the way out here to rob it?

It's like a hidden sanctuary, gracefully blending with over 7,000 square feet of rugged coastline, which I'm also assuming is the reason he chose to live here.

As I push open the heavy Oak door and enter the mansion, another flurry of wind blows up, a myriad of leaves and twigs flying past me to litter the foyer.

"Shit!" I cuss loudly, pushing the entire force of my body against the door until it eventually obeys and slams shut.

That's some gnarly wind out there.

If I didn't know any better, and judging by the dark clouds rolling in, I'd guess a storm is about to hit. Even a city girl like me can take a guess at that.

Which is about the last thing I need right now.

I don't bode well with storms.

In fact, I'm terrified of them.

I hate thunder.

I hate strong winds.

And I hate dark clouds.

When a storm hits in the city I usually spend the day in bed, hiding away from the terror. But out here there is nowhere to hide…

Come on, Claire, keep those legs steady now. Just find the billionaire and get this interview over and done with.

Fast.

"I better not end up being stuck in this place for the night," I murmur out loud, momentarily forgetting that I'm the one who isn't supposed to be in here.

"The mansion really isn't all that bad," the voice reverberates out of nowhere, a deep and gravelly tone commanding my attention.

Damn.

My heart stops…

4

Slowly I turn around to see the tall, brooding figure of Jackson Windsor barely a meter away.

He looks exactly like he does in photographs: dark hair, magnetically russet eyes, a perfectly chiseled jawline and conceited smirk.

Damn.

Even though he has scared me silly, he looks seductively sexy.

And he also looks proud to have caught me off guard.

"You scared me!" I practically shout at him, my pulse going into overdrive.

"My apologies," he says plainly, with no change in his expression. "You must be Claire Hudson...my number one fan?"

Ha.

He's witty.

Well that's something at least.

"Yes, I'm Claire," I reply cagily, extending out a hand.

He shakes it firmly, his rough hand engulfing mine. "Jackson Windsor."

"I'm sorry for just letting myself in, Mr. Windsor. I tried knocking several times…I guess you didn't hear me?"

"Ah, my apologies again," he says on the brink of a frown. "I was taking a walk along the cliffs, but do come in. And please call me Jackson."

I give a meek smile and follow him out of the foyer into the main living space.

Now that I'm inside, the lead light coming through the windows is as bedazzling as I thought it would be, a flood of sun-drenched ambience that any normal house owner would need to spend tens of thousands of dollars trying to achieve and yet could still never get it quite as perfect as this.

It's like the architect built the mansion to blend in with nature, *"bringing the outside in"* as the saying goes.

I can also see the paintings much more vividly now, each canvas as complex as the one before it.

I can't recall ever seeing a series of images that were so fascinating, the swirling tones of color all encompassing.

Even the paintings in the *Louvre* didn't grab me as much as these do.

It is obvious by the brush strokes that they are all by the same artist, a cursive white signature in the lower right hand corner of each one that I can't quite make out.

As I continue to scour the walls, my eyes fall on one painting much more harrowing than the others—a silhouette of a suited businessman carrying a briefcase, but with his heart exploding out in shards across the canvas.

But the shards are actually people, floating black figures in tribal outfits with blood dripping from their broken bodies. It's beautifully violent.

"This artwork is phenomenal," I utter thoughtfully, daring to look at him again.

His hypnotic gaze seems to be questioning my comment, a cold curiosity to it that leaves me both intrigued and highly tentative around him.

"A compliment from the ruthless journalist," he balks, offering a closed smile. "Now there's something I wasn't expecting."

A compliment?

Wait; surely he's not inferring that he's the artist…is he?

"You painted all these?" I ask, cocking an eyebrow.

Never in a million years would I have thought a billionaire like him could produce something so… melancholically moving.

"I did. Painting is how I spend most of my days now. It's liberating. We all need a cure for the things that woe us. This is mine."

A cure for the things that woe us?

What he could he possibly need a cure for?

He's a billionaire who ha the world at his feet and all before the age of thirty.

Even now that he's a recluse he still has everything that money can buy.

But hey, there's an interesting element for the story, Claire. Not only does this wicked billionaire have a dark artistic side, but also the traces of a conscience. Go figure.

As I go to probe him about the symbolism in his paintings, predominantly focusing on his portrait of the businessman, a sound like a raging squall suddenly rings out, screeching like a banshee in the rafters' overhead.

"I hope you're accustomed to bad weather, Claire," Jackson says offhandedly, whipping his head towards the roof. "This hurricane is going to be quite remarkable."

"Hurricane?" I waver, unable to hide the panic in my voice.

I feel my palms getting sweaty, my heart already skipping a few beats as my throat becomes drier.

It's worse than I thought.

Why did it have to be a hurricane on today of all days?

A simple storm I could have handled...

"Yes. They're very rare for the area, but the coastguard radioed me earlier. It's definitely on its way. Looks like you'll have to stay here tonight."

Stay here tonight?

With him?

Is this dark, scary mansion.

Oh shit.

This is bad.

The man who I consider to be partly responsible for turning a blind eye to the Marange torture camp where people are whipped, beaten bloody and even die?

He has to be joking... doesn't he?

"I could just come back tomorrow? Michosin is only a thirty-minute drive away, right? I'm sure the hotel there—"

"With all due respect, Claire," he interjects. "You won't make it to Michosin. The storm has already begun. It would be suicide to drive out in it."

The look of concern on his face seems almost genuine.

So far he's not exactly fitting the profile I've built up of him over the last two years.

"This hurricane," I stammer, "How bad are we talking? Like wind speeds of 65-70 miles per hour?"

"No. More like 90. People die in storms like this, Claire."

His statement cuts straight into my heart.

Deep into my heart.

I don't need to be reminded of that people die in storms.

I lost my older brother Troy to a hurricane when I was fifteen.

He and two of his buddies had been fishing off the coast of California when it blustered up, shifting way of course from where the bureau of meteorology had predicted it to be and drowning all three of them.

It was a freak event, like the hand of God.

I spent weeks crying into my pillow, unable to comprehend that my brother was gone.

Troy was my protector – my guardian.

He always had my back.

I still miss him every day, and I still pray for him every night.

Just the thought of a hurricane brings a tear to my eye.

Since that day I've always had a strong aversion to storms, seething uneasily each time I hear about one on the news.

I remember watching the footage of Hurricane Katrina and the destruction it caused, claiming 1,833 lives...

May they rest in peace.

"Claire?" I suddenly hear Jackson ask, his eyes hinting concern.

"What did you say?" I reply distantly, trying to push the thoughts of Troy and the hurricane away.

"Are you alright? Just before when I was talking about the guest house, you didn't seem to hear me."

"Oh...sorry. I got lost in my thoughts for a minute there. Um, what about the guesthouse?"

"It's been made up for you. You're welcome to stay there tonight. Although, you do have to cross the outside bridge to get to it, which I wouldn't recommend once the hurricane is in its peak."

"The outside bridge?"

"Yes, did you notice the river running through the middle of the mansion?"

"Indeed I did," I say derisively. "It's quite a distinct feature."

"Well, the canal is actually the Canyon River itself. There's an air bridge that connects the main house from the guest one as both were built on opposite sides of the river. So you can take your pick."

"Oh…the guesthouse should be fine," I tell him uneasily, but then secretly wish he hadn't given me the choice.

My pride says *no way* to sleeping anywhere near him tonight.

But the humbler side of me, and probably also the wiser side, says I'd be crazy to ride out the storm alone.

I really should've opted to stay in the main house with him.

Good job, Claire. You've proven yourself to be a sagacious decision maker yet again…

"As you wish," Jackson states indifferently, gesturing with his arm to a wide staircase on our far right. "I'll show you to your lodgings then."

I follow him slowly up to the second story and down a long corridor filled with antique furniture and more paintings.

I can already feel the fear flushing through me again, images of Troy treading water in a raging sea searing through my mind.

When a tree branch knocks against a window we're passing and almost shatters it, I jump and instinctively latch onto Jackson's arm, trying not to quiver.

Get a hold of yourself, Claire. This place is built like Fort Knox. Just try and relax.

"Wow. You sure don't like storms, huh?" Jackson jests, peering down at me.

I feel my cheeks redden under his solitary gaze. "No. It's, ah, a...childhood fear I never quite got over," I stutter awkwardly before letting go of his arm and stepping back away.

I consider telling him about Troy, but the less personal information we share about each other the better.

I'm not here to make friends and bond with the guy.

I'm here for the story.

Pure and simple.

When he merely sniggers and continues down the corridor, I scold myself for even agreeing to come to this god-forsaken mansion in the first place.

"This better be one hell of a scoop," I scowl out of earshot from Jackson, and make a vow to myself that hurricane or no hurricane, I will get the truth about the mines out of him.

5

The lights flicker out just as I finish settling into the guesthouse for the night.

From my bedroom window I can just make out the ruby orange glow of sunset across the water, the teal blanket chopping ferociously as the hurricane gets stronger.

I'm immediately regretting my decision again to be alone in the storm.

The hurricane isn't at its peak yet; I could make it over the air bridge easily.

But before I have a chance to way up the pros and cons of where I should stay, I hear three loud bangs on the glass front door and nearly jump out of my skin.

I rush over to open it and find Jackson half drenched and holding an umbrella, the water flowing off it torrents with the air bridge barely visible behind him.

"You should really come back over," he states sternly. "My backup generator won't kick in. It'd be safer if we stuck together tonight."

His eyes linger on me, waiting for a response.

After a minute of deliberating, I decide that he's right.

The smart thing to do is to stay together. Of course it is.

Even if he is the man that I have attacked for two years…

"Okay," I say with a quick nod, accompanied by a rigorous rumble from my belly.

I haven't eaten anything today but the sludge they gave me on the plane.

Flying first class isn't all it's cracked up to be food-wise.

The extra legroom, comfy big seats, quick service and unlimited champagne on the other hand was quite exceptional.

"I don't suppose you have anything to eat over there by any chance?" I add.

"I do, actually," he replies, grinning deviously. "I'd just finished cooking when the lights went out. I hope you like oysters Kilpatrick and smoked salmon!"

"Honestly, I could eat a horse if that's what was going," I tell him candidly, surprising even myself with my change of tone.

On the plane I'd decided to remain short and sharp with him at all times.

Strictly professional.

And yet something in those deep, bottomless eyes is daring me to do otherwise.

I think back to my conversation with Hank and the reference to me potentially seducing Jackson to get the exposé.

Am I really capable of such a thing?

I've always considered myself to be a reasonable and morally apt kind of person. *'We are what we do in this world, Claire', had been her father's motto for years, 'and if being immoral is at the core of it, then we cannot consider ourselves to be good people, now can we?'*

And yet uncovering the truth about Jackson and his mines could be seen as doing a great justice to the world.

I wonder what my father would think of my little ultimatum.

I suspect he wouldn't be too pleased if I chose the former and somewhat seductive pathway.

But then again, he's a public prosecutor, forever trying to find the injustice of a case even when it isn't there.

I leave Jackson waiting at the door whilst I go and gather up my things.

"Oh, don't be ridiculous, Claire," I gabble to myself. "You're both trapped in a hurricane. You can at least talk civilly to the guy and hear him out. Honestly, you're acting like a precious schoolgirl."

And just like a precious schoolgirl would find it hard to resist the captain of the football team, I fear I too may fall prey to my desires...

6

When we reach the house, we dry ourselves by the open fire in the main living room, surrounded by hanging deer antlers and more of Jackson's evocative paintings. We eat the oysters and smoked salmon, a bottle of ridiculously expensive Shiraz also empty on the pine wood table between us.

Up until this point the conversation has been mostly small talk: the history of the area, the architectural details of the mansion, how many hurricanes this part of Canada has witnessed in the last ten years.

But now that I'm on my third glass of wine and feeling fairly confident, I decide it's time to up the ante.

"So, my editor said you requested me to come here personally. What's the deal with that?" I ask Jackson frankly, looking him straight in the eye.

"I've read your work. You're a good journalist," he answers straightaway. "You're not afraid of exposing the *sordid* details." He holds his glass up to his lips. "That's what you think I am right? *Sordid*?"

He takes a sip of the wine, his eyes static and still on me.

I laugh weakly and polish off the rest of my glass. "*Sordid* is a strong word, Mr. Windsor."

"Indeed it is, Miss Hudson. Another wine?"

"Why not?" I retort, still mulling over the rest of my answer as I watch him get up and head down the corridor towards the wine cellar.

When he comes back with a vintage Merlot he refills both of our glasses and returns to the black leather armchair by the fire.

"So you didn't answer my question?" he gibes, staring into the flames.

If I wasn't already half buzzed, I'd find him quite intimidating, but at this very moment in time all he represents to me is a very attractive man who has information.

Valuable information.

The flickering light of the fire has cast his handsome face into harsh, angular planes, an anger blazing there I suspect that has yet to surface.

I sweep my eyes over Jackson once more; despite my dislike for him I also can't deny the sexual pull I feel towards him.

Every time I try to remind myself what a scoundrel he is, another portion of me tries to cancel it out, yearning for his lissome body and come-hither lips like an animal in heat.

I think I'm starting to come around to the idea that flirting might just be the right way to go about getting this interview.

"I don't think you're *sordid*," I say demurely, tracing the rim of my glass with my finger. "I don't know you."

"Really?" he replies speculatively. "Because many of your feature articles refer to me as *'the billionaire toy boy who endorses slave labor and torture camps.'* "

Okay…he's got you on that one, Claire.

"It's curious that the publication even prints them," he then inserts.

"Why's that?" I ask defensively, not quite sure of where he's going with all this.

"Well, the stories that have been coming out of *Leading Edge Press* lately haven't exactly be stellar reads."

"Sorry? I still don't follow…"

"There seems to be a shift away from serious new stories in your paper, Claire. If I had to take an estimated guess, I'd say that this time next year the kind of stories you choose to write about won't even be featured in it anymore."

His statement comes as a hard blow.

I knew Hank has been directing the paper away from more important news stories recently, but inferring that they'll be gone completely is a bit harsh.

"It's true that my editor wants the paper to focus more on 'pop culture' and 'sensationalism,' which honestly I can't stand to read about let alone write about. But I don't think he'd be so brash as to get rid of serious news completely."

Jackson tips his head to one side like he disagrees, the hint of a smug smirk on his lips.

"Getting back to what you said earlier though," I continue. "So you disagree with those comments then? About being a billionaire playboy?"

His face carves into a wide smile, revealing white, even teeth. "Are we on the record now, Claire?" he asks with fastened insolence.

"If you want to be," I say, batting my doe eyes at him and running my tongue provocatively across my lips.

But as far as I'm concerned, we've always been on the record.

Our eyes lock together in a contest of wills, neither one wanting to submit to the other.

I stand my ground and keep my eyes locked on him.

Even though I know he's probably just toying with me, but I'm determined to beat him, overpower him, and get the facts no other journalist has succeeded in obtaining.

And if that means a scandalous tumble in the sheets...so be it.

The story would be worth it.

"Why did you close your mines?" I inquire gently, crossing over my leg towards him.

He seems like the kind of guy who knows the fine art of body language.

Fall for the bait, Jackson. Go on.

He takes another mouthful of wine and breaks his gaze, a small victory for me as a tick of nervousness appears on his face.

"Come with me," he then orders, disregarding my question as he gets back up and walks down the corridor.

A large slice of me doesn't want to obey him.

I have a loose idea of what awaits me at the other end, as an image of a bed and Jackson stark naked loops in my mind.

"It's just for the story," I tell myself when I rise, tracing his footsteps up the dark passage.

Jackson leads me to the end of the house, stopping at a glass panorama of windows that display the violent ocean and jutted rocks below.

Okay, Claire, it's not where you had thought he was taking you. That's interesting...

"It's bittersweet," Jackson says after a few moments of silence, staring out into the violent half-lit night. "How something so raw and beautiful could also be so dark and sinister."

Much like some of your paintings, I want to say but once again lose all courage to spit it out.

As I match his gaze out the window I feel like I'm suspended in air, perched in a glass box in the middle of a wild hurricane.

Happy flipping Friday indeed, I think to myself, shuddering at the thought of the box suddenly smashing and sending the both of us down to a grisly death.

"It's rather like you, actually," Jackson resumes, head turned in my direction. "So beautiful, yet so full of…unhappiness."

I hardly believe the words when they fall out of his mouth.

Unhappiness?

I am not full of unhappiness!

How dare he say that! I'm happy…at least 90 percent of the time.

I love my lifestyle in New York: my apartment, my friends and more specifically my job, except for the Hank side of it.

"I beg your pardon?" I throw at him, anger surging in me.

If I were any drunker I'd consider slapping him in the face.

Although thinking that back over, if I'm really being honest with myself, I most likely wouldn't do something like that.

As much as my fiery temper at times otherwise suggests, I wouldn't even hurt a spider if it were crawling over my pillow; I'm one of those people who trap them in a jar and release them back outside instead.

"You don't know me," I jeer at him, whose arrogant smirk is enough to make anyone lose their cool. "How dare you insinuate otherwise."

"You claim to know who I am in your articles," he snaps wittily like he's enjoying riling me up.

"Prove me wrong then," I say, nostrils flaring whilst I straighten out my chest. "Tell me what happened in the mines."

"You're also a foolish little journalist, you know that?" he quips again, the smirk still there like a proud narcissist.

Then before I even have a chance to blink he clasps an arm around my slim waist, pulling me against him.

His free hand tangles in my hair, pulling on it so hard that I'm forced to look up at him.

He appears to be studying my face: eyes, nose and pinched lips, each distinct feature, like they hold an answer to something he's been trying to figure out.

"What the hell do you think you're doing?" I shout, struggling under his grip.

Never in my life has anyone touched me so forwardly.

Has this been his plan all along?

Asking me over here from the guesthouse...serving up oysters, a well-known aphrodisiac, and then plowing me with his fine, aged wine to get me tipsy enough to sleep with him whilst the backdrop of a hurricane rages on around us?

It's a perfect seduction, really.

I should've heeded Sophia's warning after all...

7

"Don't play coy with me, Claire. You've been batting those long, glossy eyelashes at me. I thought this was what you wanted," he says in a superior tone.

"It most certainly is not what I want," I wince, still trying to pull away from him, yet also finding it equally hard to fight the effect his hands on me is having on my libido. "Don't flatter yourself."

But Jackson hasn't seemed to hear me, lowering his face closer, and his breaths warm and infused with wine.

It shouldn't come as a great shock when he kisses me, but my body doesn't know it. His lips move easily, teasing my mouth before his tongue finally enters and collides with mine.

I stiffen instinctively, at first repelled by him and trying again to burn in my mind what a tyrant he is...the workers he's forced into labor...the torture camp he may have endorsed...but then more pleasurable sensations take over, spreading out over my body.

I haven't been laid in over six months, and the synthesis of his body against mine is bringing out a dormant desire begging to be fulfilled.

When he ends the earth-shattering kiss I am left speechless and compliant in his arms.

"So that's what malicious journalism tastes like," he whispers, his lips trailing down to my neck. "Funny, I wasn't counting on it being so satisfyingly sweet."

"You're an animal," I murmur, yet can't help but revel from the touch of his lips.

Soon they return to mine again, and willingly I open my mouth back up to him, a dizzying cloud of hunger enveloping my mind from the loss of contact with his lips only seconds earlier.

He kisses me fervently, lust now the only true north as he scoops me up into his arms and carries me upstairs to the master bedroom.

I feel vulnerable but comfortable in his strong arms.

He makes me feel like a woman that needs his care…

On his dark antique four-poster bed, draped with white Egyptian silk sheets, we embrace again, tearing our clothes off feverishly so that we're both naked under each other's ravenous gaze.

As Jackson's mouth traverses down my body I purr in his ear, "A friend warned me about you. She said you get whoever you want."

"You should have listened to her," he purrs back. "She knows what she's talking about."

He stares at me for a while before moving in to kiss me again.

Oh…

He is intoxicating.

I uncontrollably moan against his demanding lips. His hands explore my figure without constraint; he isn't timid while touching me, and it sets my body on fire.

No one has never touched me like this.

I need more.

His tongue traces my mouth before it intertwines with my own.

Yes…

He kisses me with a hunger that I've never experienced.

It's something that I've read about and have seen in the movies, but no one has ever kissed me like this. He doesn't even know me, but he's treating me like I'm the only person in his world.

For tonight, I want to pretend.

The hard bulge between us presses against my leg.

Oh… that's big.

My hand moves down his body until it reaches his cock.

Yes…

He gives a slight groan as I gently massage his hardness. I can feel the blood surging to his cock and he's getting harder with each passing second.

A deep moan escapes my lips and I feel….powerful!

Me!

I'm the one getting all of these amazing reactions from one of the hottest men I've ever seen.

His kisses move to my ear and he whispers, "You're so fucking beautiful."

I shudder against him as he kisses across my shoulder. I feel exposed and vulnerable, but it is difficult to feel insecure when he is looking at me like he's ready to consume me. I feel like a real woman. One that is desired and wanted. One that is in control.

It's downright sexy.

"Amazing…" he groans as he kisses my perky breasts.

My responding giggle quickly turns into a moan as he licks my nipple.

His hands mimic my actions from earlier, he cups my center in his large hand and massages it with his palm. I push against his hand because I love the friction it provides.

"You're so responsive," he mutters.

His mouth finds my nipple again and he begins a slow and sensual assault.

Oh…

His tongue flicks quickly over it as he holds it in place with his teeth.

Each flick of his warm velvet tongue goes directly to my pleasure center.

I'm his.

There is no mistaking it – I am his.

His fingers gently brush me before he dips his middle finger inside of my wet and waiting pussy.

Just one finger has me writhing in pleasure.

He gives it a slight wiggle and laughs lightly as I moan uncontrollably.

"You like that?" he asks in a commanding voice.

I give him a shy nod – I do like it.

A lot.

His smile is filled with lust and he dips his head between my legs.

Oh!

He sucks my aching clit into his mouth, causing me to wriggle against his face, and flex my walls around his finger.

Yes...

He presses another digit inside of me and I am lost. My body becomes alight with the flood of sexual sensation – my skin tingling with passion.

His fingers press against my g-spot as his mouth makes love to me.

From somewhere deep inside, a loud moan escapes. I have never been one to be loud in bed, but right now, I can't stop it. I can't stop anything.

This man is doing the most amazing things with his mouth and the world should know.

His mouth is mind-blowing. It's soft, warm, and firm.

I don't know what he's going to do next, he's keeping me on the edge with my next orgasm is threatening to erupt.

"Jackson," I whisper as I place my hand on the back of his head.

He speeds up his momentum and sucks hard, demanding my orgasm. His other hand travels up my body and pinches my nipple.

I am lost…

"Oooooh, I'm coming. Faster…more…please…yes…there," I plead as I press my pussy against his wanting mouth.

Suddenly, I'm not sure if I'm experiencing multiple orgasms or one long one. My body is out of control, seizing, and then releasing my pent-up frustration.

My mind is somewhere else...

As I come down from my orgasm induced high, he moves back up to me.

I grab his face between my hands and kiss him.

I can taste my sex on his lips and I don't care.

He's an excellent man, I would vote for him if he ran for president.

Anybody that can do that with their mouth deserves the very best that life has to offer.

He leans back from me and I catch a full view of his body. He is a work of art and I unashamedly stare at him.

I want to get a full view of him so that it can be ingrained in my head forever.

His chiseled chest and abs are the things that statues are made of, but his cock is the main attraction.

It's thick, powerful, and bulging.

It's bobbing up and down in twitching motions and I have to reach out and touch it.

I lay back on the bed, he joins me and nudges my knees apart with his.

He crawls between my things and begins to tease me.

Jackson moves his cock head up and down my lips. I press forward trying to take him inside of me.

He laughs at my attempts and I give a frustrated growl.

"So the journalist wants this story?" he asks.

"Stop talking. Take me," I state firmly.

"Well, I wouldn't want an angry journalist."

Then…

Oh!

Fuck!

His hard cock pushes deep into me in one swift motion.

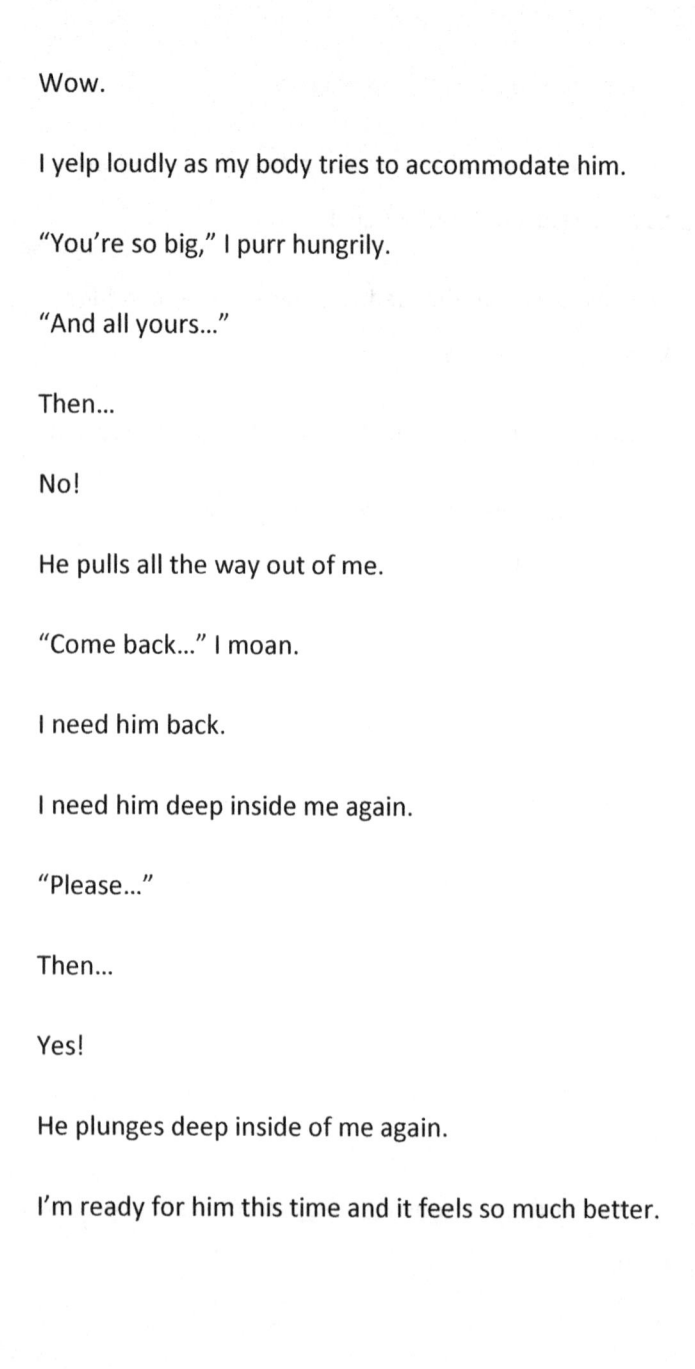

Wow.

I yelp loudly as my body tries to accommodate him.

"You're so big," I purr hungrily.

"And all yours…"

Then…

No!

He pulls all the way out of me.

"Come back…" I moan.

I need him back.

I need him deep inside me again.

"Please…"

Then…

Yes!

He plunges deep inside of me again.

I'm ready for him this time and it feels so much better.

I have never had anyone so big. He is touching me in spots that have never been touched before. He's opening me completely and with each stroke, he brings me closer to another orgasm.

"I want to feel your pussy cream all over me," he states.

I nod my head in agreement.

"No, tell me you can give it to me," he demands.

I blush because I'm not accustomed to talking dirty.

Usually, I don't say a word in bed.

He stops his movements and stares at me.

I move my hips against him, taking more of him inside of me, but he grabs my hips and holds them in place.

"Tell me," he demands again.

"I can try," I say meekly.

"No. Don't try. Do it," he says as he withdraws and thrusts into me again.

It's hard for me to stay focused on what he is saying.

I am lost in the way he is taking me.

What does he even want me to say?

"Say it," he demands.

He gives me no choice but to reply.

"Yes."

"Say it."

"I can cum all over your dick."

"That's more like it."

His pace begins to quicken and he is taking me harder than I have ever been taken.

His thrusts become deeper, the bed slams heavily against the wall but I can't give it any thought. This man is completely dominating me.

He owns me.

My pussy convulses, contracts, and I give him exactly what he wants.

I pull him close to me as my orgasm overtakes my entire body.

It floods into every part of my body and my head throws back on the bed.

Fuck.

Yes.

As another orgasm begins to calm down, he withdraws from me, "Turn over."

His deep, tough voice controls me.

My body rolls over onto my hands and knees.

He slowly trails kisses down my spine before he kisses both cheeks of my ass.

"You're so perfect," he says in a low voice.

His large hands grab my hips and he plunges deep inside of me again.

"Ooooh yes…," he moans.

"Faster," I demand as I push back against him, meeting him thrust for thrust.

The sound of his thighs slapping against my ass can be heard throughout the room.

He is pounding me with his hardness... and I love it.

He groans and grabs a hand-full of my hair, pulling it forcefully as he fucks me like I can't believe.

Then...

One last time...

He thrusts deep into my wetness.

And I am blinded by another orgasm.

Oh...

He collapses on me, and I welcome his body weight.

Eventually he rolls over and pulls me with him so that we can cuddle with each other. The warmth touch of his body feels wonderful.

I never want this moment to end.

I want this moment to last forever.

"That was incredible," I gasp, still reeling from the experience.

"You were incredible," he kisses my forehead.

In the warm embrace, I feel safe.

I feel at ease.

His warm touch feels like home.

Before long, I fall asleep while enjoying the luxury of a stranger's embrace.

8

I open my eyes and blink into the light, the curtains partly pulled open to allow a sliver of sunlight to spill into the room.

Jackson stands barefoot over by the window with only grey track pants on, the contours of his bare back daring me to be seduced all over again.

My eyes wander over the gentle V-shape that comes to a taper where his waist meets his pant line, the curve of his perfectly shaped and supple ass sitting idly in the cotton.

He seems to be staring out at the sea whose white-tipped waves I can now barely hear.

The hurricane has passed.

Thank God.

"Hey," I utter softly, slowly getting up from the bed to go and stand beside him.

I run both hands along the lithe muscles of his right arm, the skin smooth yet taut under my palms, only to find him flinch and turn sharply away from the window.

"Sorry, did I startle you?" I ask, gazing up into his eyes that look as fragile as spun glass.

"No," he replies vaguely, the whisper of a lie.

He leans down and gives me a peck on the cheek, a succession of butterflies rapidly swarming in my stomach.

Seriously, Claire? Butterflies? Remember why you're here! The story.

"How did you sleep?" he asks with a warm smile, his temperament changing completely.

"Like a log," I bray with a yawn and a stretch, pretending I haven't noticed the odd change in him.

He chuckles at my answer. "Good to hear it."

Reaching up on tiptoes I kiss his shoulder enticingly, the journalist in me reawakening.

"I think after last night's efforts I deserve a reward, don't you?" I muse at him.

"Is that so?" he queries, eyeing me suspiciously. "And pray tell what does this reward have to be?"

I hesitate before asking it.

The reporter in me is battling with a conscience, a moral tug of war ensuing that I'm not sure my conscience can win.

The story means more to me than a mere one nightstand with a billionaire, a billionaire who despite displaying some fragility still owes me for my time.

After all, he's the one who invited me here to do the interview in the first place.

Surely he understands that I need to get what I came for.

So I let the words float lightly out of my mouth, "Why did you close your mines, Jackson?"

I watch the look of disappoint stain his face. He'd been expecting me to say something else.

"Relentless little vixen, aren't you?" he says drolly, breaking away from me to stride towards the door.

"Jackson, I—"

But he cuts me off instantly.

"Just come and get some breakfast," he orders. "The power is back on, and I make a mean set of pancakes."

For about the hundredth time in less than twenty-four hours, I honestly can't tell whether he's angry or merely amused by me.

He really is a case of the Dr. Jekyll/Mr. Hyde complex if I ever saw one.

The kitchen smells of flour and sizzling butter, with a selection of bacon, sliced banana and maple syrup on the breakfast block in the middle of what has to be, at the very least, a minimum 50,000-dollar stainless steel kitchen.

"It smells amazing in here," I exclaim, taking a seat. "I've never had Canadian pancakes before."

"You're kidding?" Jackson says pompously, like it's one of the craziest things he's ever heard. "Canadian pancakes are the bomb diggity!"

"*The bomb diggity?*" I repeat, looking at him like he's a preschooler. "How old are you, like 5?"

"Sure. Why not?" comes the satirical answer, which I loosely pay a smile to; even when he's being sarcastic I still can't help but find him kind of endearing.

But that has to be the sex talking though, right?

We've been intimate now.

We've seen each other in all our pride and glory.

Barriers have been broken.

Professional barriers…and others…

"The journalist smiles. Wonders will never cease!" Jackson cries out, turning around from the stove to wink at me.

"Ha ha. Very funny," I say dryly, checking out the curvature of his ass once he's turned back around to continue frying the pancakes.

When he finally brings them over and sits down opposite me, I can't help but feel a twinge of guilt about what I'd asked him back in the bedroom.

"I'm sorry about before," I tell him, "It's just you flew me out here for an interview about the mines, and so far you haven't said anything about it."

He pours the maple syrup over his plate of steaming hot cakes, denying me all eye contact.

What is he playing at?

"You'll get your interview, Claire. Don't worry," he finally says with a solid swallow.

But when will I exactly?

I'm on the cusp of asking, and yet once again can't find the nerve to.

The towering billionaire has a strange power over me, and it's not just due to his striking good looks and athletically toned body.

It's deeper than that, deeper than the mask he's hiding behind, a sadness there that seems to be locked away in a dark sandbox that I'm desperate to open.

Something tells me that the woes he spoke of yesterday and the violence depicted in his paintings are linked to his secrets...

9

Ten minutes passes and we still haven't said another word to each other, eating our pancakes in silence.

When we both finish them I decide to break the awkwardness and go to clear the table, only to have Jackson's arm fling out and stop me.

He speaks in a chilling tone that seizes my complete attention;

"It was a stinking hot day when I got the call, which was normal for that time of year. Summer in Africa is, needless to say, awful if you're not used to it. I was in my bungalow not far from one of the mine sites in Zimbabwe. The loud crash came a minute before the call did. When I answered the phone I already knew what was I was going to hear," he pauses to take a breath, looking up at me with watering eyes.

"Three hundred people," he whispers, his forehead moving pensively like he's seeing something that I can't. "Three hundred people died on my watch that day, Claire."

I feel the goosebumps stipple on my skin, gazing over at Jackson like he's a murderer and casualty all in one fold.

"Why did the mine collapse?' I ask, keeping my voice steady.

"The structural engineers cut costs. Their design wasn't sturdy enough to support the work we were doing in there. I didn't know my company's managerial staff had approved the cheaper materials. I was too wrapped up with investing in a third mine site further into the jungle and…I…just…"

He buries his face in his hands, trying to hold back the sobs of a broken man.

I'm not sure how to respond to all this.

I feel like I'm on the edge of a precipice.

Do I jump back into reporter mode, short and sharp like I'd always planned it and play on his vulnerability to get the story no matter what?

Or do I stay on the precipice and go with a more boring interview, where Jackson doesn't get implicated in the deaths of 300 workers, and I head back to New York knowing there's a demotion waiting for me.

My dreams of career advancement obliterated.

"It wasn't your fault, Jackson," I eventually sigh, reaching out to take his hand.

In only a few minutes he's managed to reverse my entire opinion of him, an opinion that has had two long years of hate attached to it.

How could I have misjudged him so severely?

"I may not have approved those cheap materials, but it still happened under my jurisdiction," he states disdainfully. "I'm to blame. I'm responsible for all those bodies. I destroyed families."

I give him a moment before I press him further.

The last thing I want to happen is for him to go and crack on me.

*Billionaire recluse declared insane after flighty blonde reporter visits mansion...*ha, what a headline that would be!

"How did you manage to keep it out of the media?" I ask carefully, deciding that the only way I can know for sure which angle to write the story in is to hear the rest of it first.

"I paid off everyone...the survivors, the employees, and the families of the workers who died."

"And the families weren't angry? They just settled on a figure you gave them?" I add assertively, wishing I had my notepad in front of me.

Despite my struggling conscience Hank and Sophia were right; I'm literally sitting in the nucleus of a cash cow right now.

Jackson observes me somewhat peculiarly; the look on his face promoting the notion that I've asked a rather ludicrous question.

"Africa is a very different place to here. Do you have any idea how much even one hundred American dollars would mean for those miners families? Before I bought the mines the workers could barely feed their families. Some months they were on the brink of starvation, malnourished and barely clothed. They were desperate and willing to do anything for some money. That is the real Africa, Claire. The one that we western folk all too easily turn a blind eye too," he scorns.

But he's preaching to the choir.

I already know all that.

It's been a part of my job as a journalist to learn about it.

It's obvious from Jackson's countenance that he is not only ashamed of himself, but also ashamed of all the rich nations in the world who know what goes on and yet do nothing to help.

"I covered it up," he continues. "I kept it out of the tabloids and with complete radio silence. I just wanted to forget about it, so I decided to keep to myself and stay away from people. I couldn't harm anyone then."

"But, Jackson, you can't stay cooped up in this mansion either, no matter how luxurious it is. It's not healthy. It'll drive you mad," I protest, feeling an ache in my heart for how broken this once formidable billionaire now looks.

"It's already driven me mad," he chuckles shrewdly, gesturing to one of his paintings hanging on the wall above us. "I just hide it in my art, that's all."

"You need to come back to society. If the world knows your story, I'm sure they'll forgive you. You're not to blame for what happened. You may have owned the mines and employed those dubious engineers and managers, but they deliberately didn't tell you about the changes. They're the ones who should be recluses, or better yet be sent to jail for their crimes," I plead, the journalist in me wilting as I cup his face in my hands. "Come back to New York with me. Get away from here for a while."

"I can't," he utters softly, pulling away. "I can't trust people anymore. I'm better off here where I can't hurt anybody. Alone."

Jackson stands and goes to leave, stopping in mid pace to swing his head back to me.

"You should leave for the airport soon," he states coldly. "The hurricane has passed. You're free to go."

He leaves me on the verge of tears and still stunned by his revelation about what happened in Zimbabwe.

But I'd be heartless to leave him like this, anyone would be.

I can't believe he's been living with such an sinister secret, and one that has obviously been eating away at his soul. I must convince him to let it all go, to let the world hear his side of the story and judge him accordingly.

The truth always has a way of getting out.

Eventually someone will speak, and when they do Jackson will most likely come off looking like the bad guy. As a serious and passionate journalist I can't allow that to happen.

If Jackson isn't willing to come clean about the mine collapse and the miners who were killed, then he will leave me with no choice but to expose the tragedy for him.

10

As I watch Jackson's tall, dark figure walk uneasily along the cliff's edge I can't help but feel drawn to him.

I know he's on the brink of snapping, the horror of Zimbabwe stagnantly burning in his mind.

But where does that leave the interview and the story?

When I walk out to meet him the wind swipes fiercely at my face, the curls of my long sandy hair flying across my eyes.

Jackson looks up at me briefly before turning his stare back to the sea, his faraway harlequin face thawing me all over again.

"You're not thinking of jumping, are you?" I ask light heartedly, sweeping my hair to one side.

"No," he larks. "Although I'd be a liar if said I hadn't considered it once or twice in the past."

Jackson shifts his feet uncomfortably, his milky brown eyes blazing into mine.

"Back in the kitchen...that was the first time I've ever told anyone about what happened in the mine," he says. "I...strangely feel ok about it. Like it's less of a burden somehow."

I nod understandingly and rub his arm. "I'm glad. And that's why you need to join the land of living again, Jackson. You need to tell the world your story and be respected for doing so. And take your paintings with you. Put them in a gallery and show them to people. Through them they will see your pain and what all those deaths have done to you."

He looks back away and out to the sea, surveying it like he's searching for an absolution within the currents.

"They've been my only solace here," he murmurs. "Those paintings reflect the true rawness of me. I've never let anyone see them, except you. But even that was unintentional. I don't think I can expose myself like that, Claire. Not to the whole world."

"But that's what you don't get, by exposing yourself you're revealing that you're only human like the rest of us. You're not the bad guy. You hurt and bleed and feel just like anyone else. This is your chance to clear your name and stop people speculating about your past. Your paintings and the emotions you've poured into them will be great for the story."

"The story?" he asks sharply, his eyes constricting on me fiercely. "Of course...how foolish of me to forget about your damn story. That's all you really care about, isn't it? And here I was thinking maybe we..." his voice breaks off, shaking his head at the blank expression on my face.

But I wasn't even thinking about the story really when I said all that.

I may not have known Jackson for long, but I'm beginning to really care for him, and more than I probably should.

A large part of me hurts to see him so despondent.

"Jackson, I don't just care about the story. I said all that as a friend, albeit it's a very new and quick friendship. But, now that you've brought it up, we do need to talk about what I'm going to put in the feature article."

"Unbelievable!" he scoffs. "You're a reporter through and through."

"Yes I am!" I hurl at him, fed up with not only his inane comments but also the fact that he's simply refusing to hear what I'm saying. "You knew who I was before I came here. You requested me to do an interview about what happened in Zimbabwe twelve months ago. Has that suddenly just slipped your mind?"

"No, it hasn't slipped my mind!"

"Then why are you so shocked that I want to use what you've said in the story then? A story that will not only paint you in a good light but be poignant and real to people."

"Because that's not why I asked you here."

I look at him in absolute bewilderment.

What is he talking about?

Why else would I be here?

11

"What do you mean that's not why you asked me here? If I'm not here for an exposé, then what am I here for?"

Jackson gives a long, drawn out sigh, running a hand through his hair apprehensively.

"Your editor, Hank, is an old family friend. I contacted him a few days ago and told him I was lonely. He suggested I consider doing the interview. I said I would take it under advisement only if he sent you."

"Okay. But why me?"

"Because I wanted it to be someone who would tell things to me straight and judge me accordingly. What better person than the beautiful journalist who thinks I'm one of the most evil men in the world."

"I don't think you're evil," I barely whisper, tears beginning to form in my eyes, but Jackson is already walking away again, observably uninterested in anything else I have to say.

"Go home, Claire. Write what you want about me," he shouts back.

I contemplate going after him, but it's pointless.

He's made it clear how he feels.

He wants to stay here with just his canvases for company whilst the rest of the world breathes on around him.

After walking along the cliff's edge myself for a while, I manage to clear my head.

I return to the mansion with the intention of sitting down with Jackson so that the both of us can figure out a plan of action for this damn interview.

But when I find him shut away in his room, refusing to answer my gentle taps on the door, I am once torn between staying and going.

As another hour passes and only more silence from his bedroom, I choose to leave him to it.

I don't know Jackson well enough to do anything more than that.

Before yesterday I was just a stranger to him.

No, I was worse than that.

I was a stranger trying to depict him in my articles as an evil rich industrialist, hiding himself away from the world because he knew he was guilty of a crime.

But really he's just a lonely billionaire with a virulent secret that he doesn't deserve to be burdened with.

He's repented enough for what wasn't even his fault to begin with.

I scribble a note for him before I leave, carefully placing it down on the kitchen counter where I know he'll see it:

Dear Jackson,

It wasn't your fault. You're a good man. I know that sounds ironic coming for me, given our history and all, but please believe me when I say that the world will forgive you for what happened in Zimbabwe. Just as I have forgiven you for it.

Your artwork is haunting and inspirational. It deserves to be seen. Regardless of whether you show it to anyone else ever again, I hope you never stop painting.

I'm glad I got the chance to meet you. I won't ever forget the brief time we spent together.

Yours truly,

Claire

I wonder if Jackson can see the black BMW as I gradually make my way down the long and windy driveway, and back out to greater Vancouver Island.

My eyes are glued to the rear vision mirror, hoping to catch a glimpse of him from one of the windows of the second story, or see his figure running out after me, shouting that he's changed his mind.

But the strange billionaire that I have gotten to know over the last day or so never appears.

Soon the mansion becomes merely a blur, sinking back in the wooded landscape once more, an exodus that dares me to wonder if it had even existed at all.

12

One week later...

"So what are you going to do?"

Sophia is staring at me with her wide brown eyes, her cute mouse smile drawn in a theatrical round O.

"I don't know," I sigh dejectedly. "What would you do?"

But the only answer she's willing to give me is a mere shrug of her shoulders.

It's only been a week since I left Canada and Jackson's mansion by the sea, but boy does it feel like longer.

They say absence makes the heart grow fonder, but I've never truly understood that expression.

Until now.

It's not that I'm in *love* with Jackson.

I mean, how can you love someone after only a few days, right?

And more significantly how can you be in love with someone who you have loathed in the past?

There is something there though, some elusive feeling that I can't seem to shake no matter how hard I try.

Have I fallen for him?

Perhaps.

Would I be with him if I had the chance?

Possibly...

And that's about as much as I can figure out right now.

In front of me the first draft of the story glows on the computer screen, the battle now over between the journalist and her conscience, with the underdog coming out on top:

The Silent Painter

I would be the last person to say that the billionaire recluse Jackson Windsor is a good guy.

I have always said just the opposite.

Up until recently I didn't know anything else about him except for his sordid past.

A past that is laden with alleged involvements in illegal diamond mining, forced labor and torture camps. Jackson Windsor might be one of the richest and most mysterious men in the world, but the high flying and handsome tycoon also has a secret...a deep, dark secret that I was determined to uncover as soon as I stepped through the grand doorway of his lavish cedar mansion on an isolated coastline of Vancouver Island...

I'll never forget the moment when I first saw those magnificent walls, the beautiful array of canvases adorning them that had instantly taken my breath away.

There's an unusual scope of genius in his artwork that many artists only aspire to achieve.

A genius that I also hope Windsor will one day choose to share and entrust to the world.

Thus, instead of a young, greedy and guilty tyrant, I found a lonely billionaire.

His dark secret...merely an ability to paint...

And so the article goes on, everything there in full detail except for what I went to the mansion to find out in the first place.

My conscience is what ultimately swayed me.

I just couldn't do it to Jackson.

I just couldn't write the whole story without his permission.

So I published it void of the mine collapse and the deaths of the three hundred miners, focusing instead on a forlorn billionaire who prefers to live out his days as a brilliant artist in seclusion.

A billionaire whom I also hope will one day share his mastery with the rest of us, entrusting the meaning of his canvases to the world.

In the end it is Jackson's story to tell.

Not mine.

When I'd given Hank the final draft of the story along with a half forged interview transcript, I was prepared for the fallout.

I'd already decided that if he were going to demote me back to being a *'How To'* girl, then my time at *Leading Edge Press* would be over.

I'd simply walk out and never look back.

But when it came down to the crunch, Hank didn't have the balls to do it.

In fact, he barely said a word for the entire time I was sitting in his office.

He just took the story from me, made a few grammatical corrections and an extra paragraph break, and then handed it back.

Not one comment on its content.

It was very un-Hank like and rather unsettling, to be honest.

"Maybe Hank's wife left him?" Sophia suggests, handing me the mug of steaming hot coffee.

We're taking some time out on one of the lime green sofas to find our "inner inspiration." Well, that's what we're masking our gossip session as anyway.

"No. I don't think it's that," I say, blowing on the coffee before taking a sip. "I got the impression it was something work-related. He didn't seem sad, just indifferent. It was weird."

"Yeah, it sounds it. I haven't seen him this morning yet, but he cancelled the staff meeting for today."

"What? Why?"

"No idea. He just sent an email saying there were changes happening and it was TBC."

Changes happened?

To be confirmed?

Hank didn't mention any of that earlier.

What the hell is going on?

I'm about to question Sophia further about it when I notice him like a shadow out of the corner of my eye.

No, it can't be.

Not here.

13

"Whoa. Is that who I think it is?" I hear Sophia ask, but I'm already standing, the tall and navy blue pinstripe suit gaiting towards me.

He stops just a few steps away, his warm hazel eyes beaming at mine.

"Hello, Claire," he states indubitably, a classic smirk carved on his lips.

It takes me a few moments to process that he's really here, that he's really towering in front of me in all his handsome grandeur.

"Hello, Jackson," I say softly, unable to break away from his cavernous gaze. "What are you doing here?"

"I wanted to stop by and ah—" he pauses when he notices Sophia eavesdropping on the couch behind me, along with about ten other people who are dotted around the communal workspace.

"I wanted to see if you were free for lunch," he continues in a lower octave.

Lunch?

Something tells me he hasn't flown all the way over from Canada just for that.

"Lunch? Um...sure. Wait. No, I can't," I sigh. "Hank won't let me. He's a real stickler for breaks outside allocated hours."

"Oh that's not a problem," Jackson says with a toss of his head. "Hank's been fired."

"What? Hank's been fired? How do you know that?"

"Because I'm the one who fired him."

"But, how could you possibly have been able to do that?"

"Because I bought the paper."

"You bought the paper? As in this paper, *Leading Edge Press*?"

"Yes, Claire," he says, the grin on his face making me feel a little stupid, although, on the other hand, I had absolutely no idea that any of this was even going on.

I throw him a look of open confusion. "Sorry, I'm not sure I'm processing all this right. I thought Hank was an old family friend of yours?"

"He is."

"So why would you fire him?"

"It wasn't a personal decision, Claire. It was business. He wasn't the right fit for here. You said back at the mansion that you didn't like the direction he was taking the paper in. It turns out a few other managerial staff members didn't either. So I negotiated with the owner and here we are. I thought you'd be happy about the change?"

"I am. But, I mean...it's just that...Hank was a good editor. I don't think he deserved to be fired."

"Don't you worry about Hank. I gave him a job at another magazine I own – he'll be fine. And it's better than anyone else would have offered him."

"Right," I nod, still letting it all sink in.

No more Hank.

No more sexism.

No more old-school ways of thinking affecting the news stories.

Wow, things will certainly be different around here.

"So who's running the paper now. You?" I ask Jackson hesitantly.

"Me? Run a paper? I don't know the first thing about journalism let alone how to be an editor. I was going to offer you the job actually," he pronounces, his eyes dancing on mine.

"Me?" I practically squeak. "Are you serious?"

"Deadly," he says with a wink.

"And so I'll just be corresponding with you via video link from Canada?"

"From Canada? Oh, I won't be in Canada."

I feel my heart drop into my stomach.

He won't be in Canada?

Why?

Where's he going?

"I'll be here in New York," he carries on. "I'm moving back here, Claire."

I feel the relief surge through me instantly, a wide smile carving onto my face.

"You're moving to New York?" I reiterate, making sure I've heard him right so I don't get my hopes up.

"Yes."

"Why? I mean, what made you change your mind?"

"You," he states clearly, like he suddenly doesn't care who can hear us. "You were right about me being too cooped up in that mansion. It wasn't good for me. I was long overdue for a breather."

"It makes me really happy to hear you say that," I tell him, still beaming from ear to ear.

"I'm going to hold an art exhibition too in a couple of months. I'm going to *'entrust my genius to the world'*."

"You ready my article?" I laugh at him, my jaw starting to get sore from all the smiling.

"Of course I read your article. What do you think got me on the plane over here in the first place?"

He takes a step forward to fill the space between us, tenderly cupping my face in his hands and gazing deeply into my eyes like he's finally found what he's been searching for in them.

"So how about that lunch date, Miss Hudson?"

14

Two months later...

There's a painting hanging in the gallery that I haven't seen before.

A languid and ethereal blue hued image of a woman with long golden hair and only a bed sheet draped over her.

Her head is turned away so that you can only see a side profile of her face, whilst a four-poster antique bed sits in the background.

"It's you," Jackson whispers in my ear, enfolding his arms around my waist.

I smile and tilt my face up to his.

"I guessed that," I reply silkily before softly kissing him. "It's beautiful. When did you paint it?"

"I started it the day you left the mansion. I figured if I couldn't get you out of my head, then the next best thing was to take all those thoughts and just...draw them."

I look around at the multitude of Jackson's paintings, the light and dark images that have captivated almost everyone in here.

From New York's highest elite to New York's hippest youth, all different levels of society have come to the gallery to see the emotions bleeding from his canvases.

Last week he'd held a press conference and come clean about the mine collapse.

He'd told it to the American public much the same way as he'd told me that morning back at the mansion – *in his own words*.

He didn't hold back on the waver in his voice, or the water in his eyes, or his deep regret over the three hundred miners who had died on his watch.

And just like I thought they would, the majority of the world seemed to forgive him, calling for justice to be brought to those executive staff and engineers who were negligent.

But Jackson's answer to them was that all wrongs had already been rectified.

The families involved were rightly compensated for their loss, the guilty employees' contracts terminated and profiles blacklisted, and the mines shut down in the necessary and standard protocol.

Jackson had also revealed at the conference the meaning behind his paintings and the comfort they had given him over the dark period in his life.

In them hid his pain over the miners' deaths that had cost him some of his humanity.

People had come in droves to the gallery after that conference, hundreds upon hundreds of people interested in what this billionaire recluse had to offer in terms of not just his artistry but his empathy, remorse and ultimate salvation through painting.

"None of this would be here if it wasn't for you," Jackson says, his hands tightening on my waist.

There's a profound sincerity in his eyes that I haven't witnessed before.

We've been dating for just over two months now, and in that time I've come to know him even more intimately.

There aren't a lot of faces of his that I don't recognize.

"I owe you everything, Claire," he then utters quietly. "You're my only inspiration now. And I'm so completely in love with you because of that."

I give his hands a loving squeeze and feel the tears welling up.

I can't remember the last time I ever felt this happy.

Every now and then I have to pinch myself to make sure I'm not still lost up there in the clouds.

"I'm so in love with you too, Jackson," I say, trying not to choke up.

As we hug each other close I think back to the days when Jackson Windsor was just a jerk in one of my articles, a villain who I would spend hours upon hours trying to dig up dirt on.

And all the while he'd been nothing of the sort, hiding away in his glorious mansion by the sea, painting his sorrow in beautiful sketches and crying into the night as the nightmares of his time in Zimbabwe gripped him.

I said once that the two of us together was completely out of the realms of possibility.

But as he kisses me again, I realize that we were meant to be…

15

After the highs of the gallery opening, we end up back at his inner-city penthouse apartment. Both of us are buzzing at the success of his paintings...

When we inevitably reach the bedroom, he reaches out and strokes my face, "This feels right."

I close my eyes and lean into his hand.

I can't believe all this has happened to me.

It is unbelievable.

The man I attacked for so long has become the man of my dreams.

"Why me?"

The question just comes out of my mouth without thought.

He blinks a few times, "Pardon?"

"Why me?" I repeat myself.

"I don't understand," he shakes his head confused.

"You can have any woman you want, why me? Why choose me above everyone else?"

He shakes his head, "That's a strange question after the night we've had."

"I just feel like this is it... this is our future now," I try to explain myself.

"I wanted you because... because there was something real about you. Something that said that you weren't blinded by the money. You didn't care about my reputation or my money. You attacked me right from the start. I wanted to meet you because I knew that your reaction to the truth would be real. It wouldn't be blinded by anything else. And then after we met..."

"Yes?"

"After we met, I was blown away. Not only are you beautiful and have the greatest smile I have ever seen, but you were... genuine. I felt like there was something between us right away. I don't know what it was but I know that it made my heart beat faster than it does after a session in the gym. And that was just the start."

"Go on," I smile.

"These last two months have been the best two months of my life. With you, I feel like I can be the real me. I don't have to put on a disguise and pretend to be someone I'm not. I don't have to live up to someone's expectation about what I should be."

"That's beautiful," I whisper.

"With you, I can be me."

Those words make my heart melt.

It is the most perfect sentence I have ever heard.

"With you, I can be me," he repeats himself and I almost collapse on the spot.

He grabs my neck and pulls me in for a kiss. It's the sweetest kiss that I've ever known. It sends me to another place.

His lips are filled promises of a future that will blow me away.

The kiss intensifies and I become lost in the passion.

Our hands race over each other as the passionate kiss becomes hotter and hotter. Our embrace becomes a wrestle as we tear the clothes off each other. Quickly, we are in a naked embrace.

Yes.

Time for talk is over.

It is now time for action.

He lies on his back and I marvel at his stunning body again. Abs, chiseled chest, strong arms... delicious.

And then there's his member...

It's so big and beautiful and he's already standing upright.

My body comes over the top of his and I play with his nipples as I stare at him.

I can't help but grin as I enjoy this body.

There are so many places I want to touch and play with and right now he's all mine.

His length rests against my stomach and I stroke it with one of my hands. He groans deeply with a massive smile stretched across on his face.

"Sensitive today?" I ask playfully.

"I need you," he moans.

My hand gently brushes up and down his piece and he continues to groan. I love that I can do this to him. I love it that I make him this hard.

"I have been wanting your beautiful body from the moment I saw you tonight. I wanted to pull you into the bathroom in the gallery and fuck you senseless."

"You should have stayed." I grin.

I lower myself down his rock-hard body and wrap my warm lips around his cock. The blood practically surges to the tip.

"Ooooh... Your mouth... that mouth," he groans as he grabs my hair.

I take more of him inside of my mouth, not wanting to tease him mercilessly this time around.

It feels so good to have his hardness in my mouth.

I take as much of him as I can inside and move my tongue across his shaft.

His grip tightens on my hair and he pulls me up, "Yes. Fuck yes. Yes Claire. That's it."

My tongue dances around his tip and he almost jumps off the bed. I love that I can do this to him. I love that I have the ability to make him uncontrollable with desire.

"I need you," he moans.

"Say please," I tease him.

"I need you... please."

"That's better," I smile and I move up his body, slowly drifting my breasts over his skin. With each touch, he seems to be getting harder.

I straddle his body and gently rub my wetness over the tip of his cock.

"Please," he begs me.

"As you wish," I exhale as I slowly slide down his pole.

My body immediately reacts as it's stretched.

Yes...

I settle on his hardness for a few moments and let my pussy adapt to his hugeness.

Then, it begins.

Oh yes, it begins.

It doesn't take us long to get into the rhythm. We lose ourselves in one another.

There is a sensitivity between, it's the same sensitivity that he showed me the first night we were together, but it's amplified.

He flips me over on the bed, and withdraws from me. Standing at the end of the bed while I lie waiting, his eyes adore my body.

The way he looks at me makes me feel amazing.

There is desire, passion and lust in his eyes.

When he looks at me, I have never felt more like a woman.

I feel erotic.

While lying on the bed, Jackson's large body comes over the top of me, and I look up to his beautiful face.

Again, he stares at me.

This time, he is not staring at my body but into my eyes.

And not just my eyes…

He is looking at me.

The real me.

When his hard cock touches my wetness again, it jolts me back to reality. His hardness easily slides back into me.

Deep.

Yes…

He holds in me for a few moments and I can feel it pulsating inside me. He is throbbing with passion.

With Jackson inside me, I feel whole.

I feel complete.

As he holds his cock deep inside my pussy, he gazes into my eyes again.

My heart melts as I look deep into his gorgeous eyes.

Wow…

This feels right. This feels real. This feels...

Yes...

Jackson slowly withdraws and smoothly enters me again.

Oh yes...

As he slowly withdraws and enters me again, I run my hands over his perfect body. My hands easily smooth over his strong muscles, brushing against his skin.

I love touching his body.

It is perfect in every way.

Again he slowly withdraws and enters me again.

He is so deep.

"Take me," I plead with him.

"Tell me what you want," he demands from me.

"I want you to take me hard," I demand.

It feels so good to demand what I want.

It feels so good to be a strong, confident woman that knows what she wants.

"Harder," I demand.

He smiles with a mischievous grin that tells me this is going to be wild...

Slam!

"Yes!" I scream with surprise.

Slam!

Suddenly, Jackson is pounding me with his assertive strength. His whole body forces down onto mine, thumping my butt into the bed. He is so strong and powerful that I feel helpless under his dominance.

Helpless, vulnerable... but cared for.

Loved.

The thrusting continues.

"Yes Jackson! Yes!" I scream.

Jackson becomes quicker.

"Fuck yes!!"

And deeper.

Yes! Yes! Yes!

Harder!!

From deep inside, I can feel a moan beginning.

It starts deep within my body and gets stronger and stronger.

I can't hold it in.

I bring my arm around the back of Jackson's neck and try to keep the moan quiet.

But Jackson keeps slamming me.

I can't contain it!

As I hold onto him tightly, I let it out of my lips.

"Yes…" the moan enhances my approaching orgasm.

Wow…

I hold onto Jackson tight as he continues to thrust deep into me. I am lost in his body. Lost in his aggressive pounding.

Yes!

Beauty touches every part of my body, my head lost in dizziness.

Oh…

The world around me becomes brighter – lighter – as Jackson continues thrusting with strength, slamming himself into me with a consistent pattern. My head is spinning.

This is my moment.

I deserve this.

Yes!

His desire is saturating.

His passion is drenching.

The lust is overwhelming.

Jackson's strong hands push down on my shoulders, holding me still as he rides into me.

He has taken control of me and I am all his.

In this moment, I have no control.

Jackson slows his thrusting and I come back to reality.

I look up to him and see a smile stretched across his face.

He stops thrusting and then withdraws from me.

My chest is panting as he watches over me.

"You are the most perfect person I have ever met," he whispers.

I can't respond to him - I am too high from the orgasm.

I wait for him to return.

Please.

Fuck me again.

I need it.

Slowly, his comes back over my body. His hardness touches my pussy and slides back in.

Gently.

Then…

Slam!

He thrusts again!

"Yes!" I can't help the scream that escapes my lips.

His hard cock drives deep into my pussy, pounding me with passion.

I am lost in his rhythm.

Orgasm rushes over me again…

Flooding me like a river.

The world becomes light again...

My head is spinning...

He continues to pound into me...

Oh...

Yes...

My nails dig into his skin.

I am primal as the orgasm catches me again.

I feel his climax coming.

He grows louder and slams harder.

Then...

Oh...

He reaches his peak...

Oh...

It ends...

Jackson slowly stops thrusting and falls next to me on the bed. I cuddle into his warm body and his strong arm wraps around me.

Yes.

The warm embrace is perfect.

And it is everything I ever wanted...

The End

Emily's Note:

Thank you for reading 'The Billionaire CEO.' I really loved developing this story!

My special thanks goes to Lara, Mel and Cara. These amazing women developed this story from an idea to what it is today. I am so lucky to have these remarkable people in my world.

If you enjoyed this story, please check out my last story, 'The Assistant'.

Life has thrown some very hard times at me, but telling stories is one thing that brings me so much joy.

It is my escape.

Thank you so much for enabling me to do what I love.

I hope Jackson entertained you!

Thank you!

Emily xx

Other titles by bestselling author Emily Cooper:

Romance: Seduced by the Billionaire's Lust

Romance: The Billionaire's Assistant

Romance: Bought for the Billionaire's Pleasure

Romance: Alpha Stepbrother

Romance: The Billionaire Proposal

Romance: The Assistant

Bonus Chapter:

Romance: The Assistant

Emily Cooper

Beau Donovan exercises control in nothing; he is impulsive, filled with desire and driven by lust... until the day that Harper Clark falls into his office; full of shy, innocent looks.

Unlike any woman he has known before, Harper seems to see right through him - past the sporting talent, the rock-hard abs and the penthouse lifestyle to Beau's cold, lonely heart.

Will Harper's delicate touch open him up... or force him to run away forever?

Chapter One

"Oh, wow."

Harper's mouth dropped open as she flicked through the old magazine in the doctor's office. Her eyes landed on an underwear ad of half-naked sports star, Beau Donovan.

"Hmmm…" moaned the woman on the seat next to her. "I could run my tongue up those rock hard abs any day of the week."

"Oh no, I wasn't… I mean… I didn't…" Harper flushed with embarrassment.

"No need to be embarrassed, honey," the woman smiled. "We can all appreciate greatness."

Filled with complete embarrassment in the busy waiting room, Harper quickly closed the magazine and placed it on the table in front of her. The woman next to her picked up the magazine, flicked to the advertisement featuring the large package of Beau Donovan, and started making moaning sounds.

"Hmmm…" the woman moaned. "Yes please."

Harper's cheeks blushed with redness. After at least two minutes of deep moaning, the woman placed the magazine back on the table, much to Harper's relief.

Harper could have quietly stared at the picture for hours, and she could have done with the enjoyment, but to avoid any further unwanted embarrassment, she didn't pick the magazine back up.

Things had changed lately for Harper and life was becoming more stressful by the day, but New York City was always in a hurry to change someone's life.

Whether they were drawn to the city by the lure of fame and fortune or the temptation of the cultural explosion that was rocking the city and bringing new trends into existence by the hour, there was something for everyone from business and trade to the big screen and the top restaurants in the world.

They say if you can make it in New York, you can make it anywhere.

Eight years ago, Harper Clark had moved to The Big Apple to pursue a career in financial advising with one of the top firms in the nation and had found herself in a growing economic boom that afforded her the kind of life she had always imagined for herself and her boyfriend and hopefully soon-to-be husband.

But things tend to change quickly here.

Really quickly.

The markets changed overnight and instantly people lost their jobs and money just as quickly as they had earned it.

Harper wondered what that said about them. If the saying is 'If you can make it in New York City you can make it anywhere,' and you flop, did that mean you were considered a failure?

To live here you had to be tough and have a thick skin and the ability to bounce back when things didn't go the way they were anticipated to. Harper wasn't sure how much bounce she had left after so many things fell out from under her.

Harper stared out the window behind her, looking out to the expanse of the city, wondering how her life had taken such a turn and ended up the mess that it currently was. There were so many things that had changed over the last few months and none of them seemed to be for the better.

She crossed her legs and rested her head on the cool glass watching the cars and taxis go by on the busy street, wishing she had somewhere to be other than sitting in the cramped little doctor's waiting room. She was there because she was having a lot of trouble sleeping at night. Her brain couldn't switch off and let her sleep peacefully.

Harper was determined to get her life back in order and keep a positive outlook on things. She refused to let a few turns of bad luck and a few bad choices ruin everything.

If things could go south in a hurry, they could turn around the same, right?

She was newly single, had her own apartment and a lot of free time on her hands to venture out into the world and find her passion.

She wondered if the stock market was where she belonged.

Maybe something else would come up and she would find that she liked that better than working on the trading floor. She had some time to figure it all out, though not as much time as she would have liked and been comfortable with.

The truth was that her boyfriend of the last two years had dumped her and left her high and dry.

He took her credit cards and decided to go on a spending spree before heading out of the country to Mexico with his new girlfriend who he had proposed to with a ring he had bought with Harper's money.

To further add insult to injury, he had chosen her birthday as the ideal time to drop that bomb on her.

She was forced to move into a small one-bedroom apartment in a 'up and coming' neighborhood. Which meant that it was a slum that the city was trying to revamp before they completely lost it to poverty.

They were building new apartments and tearing down a lot of the abandoned buildings in the area in an effort to clean it up.

It wasn't the best area and it certainly wasn't the kind of place she had grown accustomed to living on the Upper East Side where people took care of their lawns and children played in their yards and everyone looked out for each other.

She wasn't even sure who her neighbors were here.

Nobody had introduced themselves and it seemed like most of them never left their apartments. Harper wondered if any of them even worked. Not that she was contributing much to society at this point.

As for having a lot of free time, she only had free time because she had lost her job shortly after moving into the new apartment.

The company she had worked for since moving to the city had needed to enforce cutbacks to keep their doors open and one of the positions they eliminated was hers.

She thought a few years of paper pushing and number crunching were going to give her an exemption from the cuts but that wasn't the way the cards fell.

Harper could have sulked about the whole situation but she decided it wasn't worth it to be negative. It wouldn't get her anywhere and it would only upset her more.

Things could only get better from here.

Mostly because that was the only option left.

Chapter Two

Harper had landed an interview with the Warrior's soccer team as a financial advisor and accountant. She hadn't done accounting beyond her internship when she left Ohio State University but she was sure the team accounts wouldn't be difficult to follow when she was used to handling dozens of accounts on a daily basis.

She hoped when they interviewed her they wouldn't ask if she liked the team.

Harper had never been much of a sports fan and she honestly couldn't remember the last time she had ever watched a soccer game or even a partial game for that matter and she wasn't confident that she could fake her way through it with someone who actually knew what they were talking about.

She pulled up in the parking lot and drove down the aisle looking for a spot that didn't have a reserved sign on it.

Harper parked her car next to a spot reserved for Beau Donovan.

The name sounded halfway familiar, like she may have seen something about him at some point.

Thinking about it she remembered that he was the party boy of the team, fantastic player with a long history of bringing the team to victory but he had been in trouble over the years with drinking and women.

Harper gave serious thought about moving her car but one glance at her watch told her she was running close to late as usual and didn't have time to be worried about which of the pretty party boys she was parked next to.

When she entered the building, there was an attractive young blonde woman at the front desk who asked if she had an appointment with someone.

She looked friendly and smiled at her.

"Yes, I have an appointment with a Mr. Edwards," Harper told her, smiling back.

"Thank you. You can have a seat and I'll let him know that you're here," the receptionist said and picked up the phone.

Harper looked around the building.

It was obvious that it had once been a very nice place but that years of hard use and the lack of money to fix it up had let it drift into a state of minor disrepair.

The carpets had stains and were getting threadbare in the high traffic areas.

It might have been blue a decade or so ago.

Everything was clean even though it wasn't in the best shape. The place looked comfortably well worn in and it smelled like a combination of cologne and industrial floor cleaning solution.

"Miss? Mr. Edwards will see you now," the receptionist smiled with beautiful teeth. She led Harper down the hallway to a room where an old man with balding hair was waiting for her.

"Welcome, Miss Clark. I'm Roger Edwards, owner of the Warriors. It's a pleasure to meet you." The man offered her a seat in one of the leather chairs in front of his desk.

"Thank you, sir," Harper sat down on the overstuffed chair and pulled her resume out of her briefcase and handed it to him.

They went over her resume and he asked her questions about her financial history and her educational background. He was also a Buckeye alumni and Harper had a feeling school bloodlines were a strong pull with this man.

"Can you please describe a time when you had a positive impact on an organization?" Mr. Edwards asked.

"Yes, I…"

Knock. Knock.

There was a heavy knock on the door as Harper began to detail her reply.

Turning to look at the man, Harper's breath was taken away.

She couldn't finish the rest of her sentence.

"Hey, Mr. Edwards, Johnny wants to know if there is anything else you need him to do to get ready for the trip on Saturday."

A tall man in his mid thirties came in looking like he had just walked off a Sports Illustrated shoot with his chiseled body and gorgeously manly face. Clearly full of confidence, he didn't care that he had just interrupted a job interview.

Harper couldn't take her eyes off him – she had never seen someone so beautiful, confident and styled.

The man had thick and luscious dark brown hair that waved in the thin layer of gel he applied to it. His strong face had the hint of stubble that had already grown back after he shaved this morning. He had muscles on top of his muscles and a stunningly broad chest.

He looked every bit the athlete he was.

Dressed beautifully in a well-fitting and stylish suit, he looked irresistible.

Harper resisted the urge to brush her hands over his chest – deciding that wouldn't be the best look in a job interview.

The man smiled over at Harper and she felt the heat rise into her cheeks when her eyes met his. He definitely had the kind of charm that a woman would fall for.

"Not now, Donovan. Can't you see I'm conducting an important interview right now?" Mr. Edwards stood.

"New assistant?" the man asked with raised eyebrows.

"Financial advisor and accountant," Harper smiled.

"Team assistant," Beau winked.

Shaking his head, Mr. Edwards shooed him out of the door, before closing it. Then, thinking about something, he opened it and stuck his head out and told the man to check with the travel agency about the hotel reservations.

"I'm sorry about that. It's always busy around here," Mr. Edwards shook his head and took his seat behind his desk again.

He sat down in his office chair and looked over her resume again, flipping through the pages and chewing on his bottom lip.

The way he was going over her resume made her nervous.

Harper knew she had good references, a wonderful work history and impressive recommendations, but the way he was inspecting the details of her career and life made her feel like there was something she was missing out on.

"If you think you can put up with an office full of guys like that…" he pointed with is thumb to the door indicating where the handsome guy had vanished "…then you can start Monday morning."

"Really?" Harper asked in surprise.

Mr. Edwards nodded.

"Oh! Thank you, sir. Thank you for the opportunity, Mr. Edwards," Harper was ready to sing.

He stood and shook her hand, "Monday morning at eight o'clock. The receptionist will tell you where to go."

Harper walked out of the office floating on clouds.

In a daze, she came around one of the hallway corners and ran straight into a solid chest.

"Oh," she yelped as her hands went onto the chest, "Sorry."

"Well, hello. If you wanted to touch my chest you could have just asked. Someone pretty as you, I'd let you touch anything you wanted," the man winked with a smile.

"Sorry," Harper said again.

"Your hands are still on my chest," he grinned.

"Oh! Sorry," Harper blushed, letting out an awkward, forced laugh.

The man was hot but completely arrogant.

"Beau," he held out his large, strong hand.

"Harper," she replied as his hand engulfed hers.

"That was you in the interview, wasn't it?"

"Um... yes."

"So did you get the job?" Beau asked Harper as she made her way around him in the hall.

She couldn't help the smile that spread over her face.

"I did," she told him.

"Good. I'll be looking forward to seeing much more of you," his smile would have erased all of the memories of his arrogance if she had let it.

She couldn't keep herself from being just a little bit charmed by the guy. His charisma was overflowing and his personality lit up the room.

He would be the life of the party anywhere he went.

Her body was working against her mind when it came to the warning signs and red flags of this guy.

She could tell he was no good.

He was trouble – no doubt about it.

And she could tell he wasn't her type... but she'd be damned if she didn't want to kiss him and find her way down those beautiful lines of his body.

"Lovely to meet you, Harper. It's always good to have more pretty girls around here. I'll see you around."

Harper smiled and her wobbly legs walked out the doors.

"Nice butt," Beau whispered as she disappeared through the doors, watching her go. "Yum."

Beau wanted to get his hands on those gentle curves.

"You look confused," one of Beau's team members walked past.

"Uh?" he hadn't realized he was in a daze.

"You're standing there, staring at nothing."

Reality sank into Beau and he realized that Harper was long gone, and he had been in a daze about the girl.

But what was it about Harper that made him want to forget everything but the way her gorgeous green eyes looked up into his and the way she smelled like strawberries in June and looked like she could melt the ice caps with that body of hers?

The curves on her body put other women to shame.

"Hot damn," he mumbled as he walked away from the doors.

Romance: The Assistant

Emily Cooper

Buy now!

Available on Kindle and in Paperback!

Made in the USA
Monee, IL
24 August 2019